# The Theology of Sci-Fi

The Christian's Guide
to the Galaxy

by
Scott L. Smith, Jr.

The Theology of Sci-Fi:
The Christian's Guide to the Galaxy
by Scott L. Smith, Jr.
Copyright © 2020 Holy Water Books

ISBN-13: 978-1-950782-26-0
All rights reserved.
Holy Water Books (Publisher)

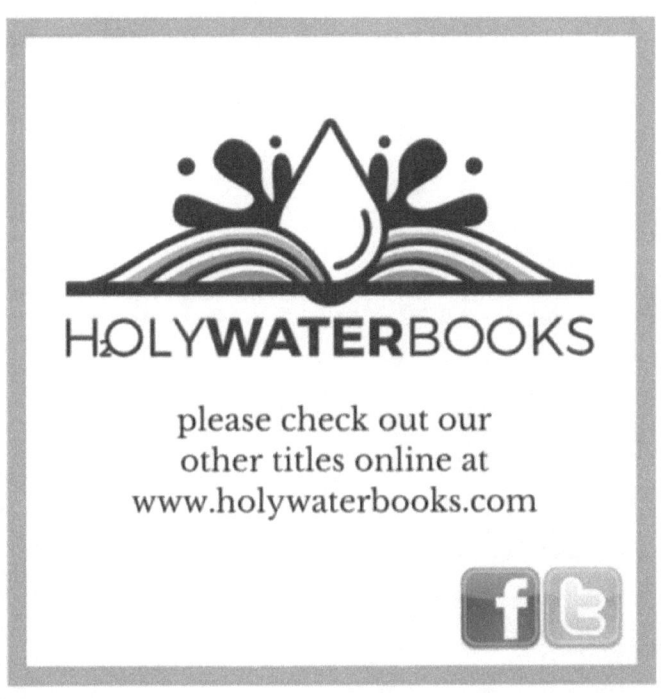

HOLYWATERBOOKS

please check out our
other titles online at
www.holywaterbooks.com

"Refusing to let God enter into all aspects of human life amounts to condemning man to solitude. He is no longer anything but an isolated individual, without origin or destiny. He finds himself condemned to wander through the world like a nomadic barbarian, without knowing that he is the son and heir of a Father who created him through love and calls him to share his eternal happiness. It is a profound error to think that God came to limit and frustrate our freedom. On the contrary, God comes to free us from solitude and to give meaning to our freedom. Modern man has made himself the prisoner of reason that is so autonomous that it has become solitary and autistic."

- Robert Cardinal Sarah

# The Theology of Sci-Fi

## Table of Contents

# Introduction

We will fold space using the spice mélange to travel from "a long time ago in a galaxy far, far away" to the planet Krypton, from Trantor to Terminus, and back to the scorched skies of earth.

Did you know there is a Virgin Birth at the core of Star Wars? A Jewish Messiah of Dune? A Holy Family in Superman? A Jesus and Judas in The Matrix? And the Catholic Church is Asimov's Foundation?

This book covers a lot of territory. It spans galaxies and entire universes. Nevertheless, we will see that the great expanse of human imagination will forever be captivated by the events of the little town of Bethlehem.

Joseph Campbell was *so* close. The author that so captivated George Lucas as he was creating the Skywalker saga of *Star Wars* was so close to a complete theory. In *The Hero with a Thousand Faces* (1949), Campbell laid out his theory of the journey of the archetypal hero shared by world mythologies. Campbell called it the "Monomyth".

But why should there be a Monomyth at all? And Who is the Monomyth? These are the answers that Campbell, a former Catholic, stopped shy of answering.

As we go over some of the greatest stories every told, hopefully the answers will become obvious. Our stories are great to the extent that they point us to the "Greatest Story Ever Told": Jesus' life, death, and resurrection.

At the heart of the Monomyth is a man, a very *real* man. The God-Man. The source and summit of all hero stories and myths ever told, both before and after those short 33 years in First Century Israel.

There is a reason that all of mankind's stories overlap, coincide, correlate, and copy. Like it or not, all mankind bears the same indelible stamp, the mark of Christ. Why should there be a singular story binding us all? Unless we are truly all bound together as one human family. At the core of the Monomyth is not another myth, a neat coincidence, but a reality—the reality of Jesus Christ.

# The Theology of *Star Wars*

The impact of Christianity on the mind of George Lucas is undisputed. The Jedi are basically monks with lightsabers.

I will focus the discussion of the theology of *Star Wars* on two main topics: (1) the Virgin Birth of *Star Wars*, and (2) the Jedi and the Communion of Saints.

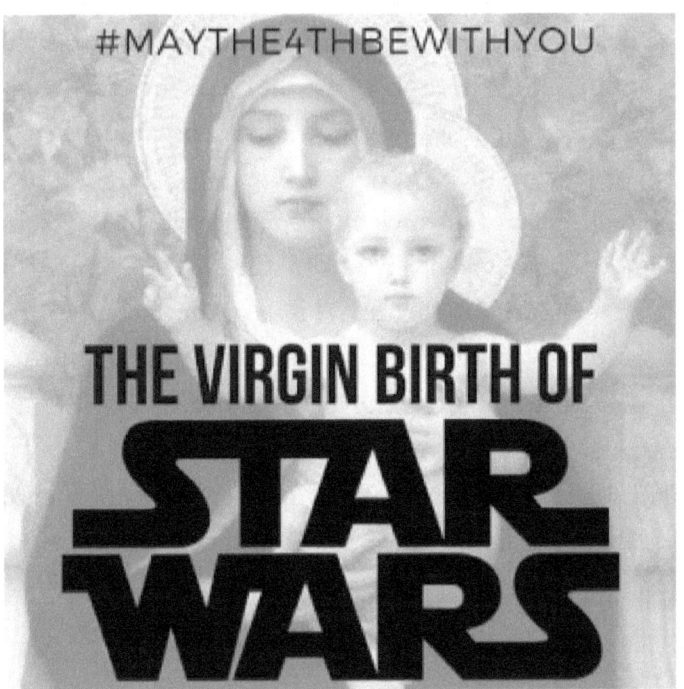

# The Virgin Birth of Star Wars

I'm pretty sure I first watched *Star Wars* in the womb. I'm pretty sure that the first time I heard the trumpet blast of the score of *A New Hope*, I was encased in amniotic fluid. I was actually born the day after *Return of the Jedi* was released.

It is such sweet satisfaction to know that the amniotic origins of *Star Wars* were also Catholic.

We should probably expect this from a series of movies in which the heroes are running around in cassocks like a Capuchin monk. The robes of the Jedi are the robes of Catholic monks. Instead of rosaries hanging from their belts, the Jedi have lightsabers.

The Jedi speak of an ancient prophesy that is fulfilled by the birth and life of Anakin Skywalker. Clearly, the subject of the prophecy is a Messiah figure. This is made blatantly obvious when we discover that he is the seed of woman (Gen 3:15) alone, that he was **conceived by the Force,** that Shmi gave birth as a virgin.

*Hello, McFly!* This is one of the most obvious connections in all the galaxies in all the universes of science fiction.

# The Prophesy of the Chosen One

*"You refer to the prophecy of the one who will bring balance to the Force. You believe it's this…boy?"*

Mace Windu

The Prophesy of the Chosen One spoke of the coming of a savior who would bring balance to the Force. It was also referred to as the Prophecy of the Son of the Suns. The Chosen One was also referred to as the Son of Suns. Sound familiar? The King of Kings?

Also, speaking of "suns", remember the iconic image of Luke contemplating his destiny before the setting Twin Suns of Tatooine?

And then the blare of the lone trumpet as the "Force Theme" is played during the binary sunset:

And the same shot again with baby Luke in the arms of Uncle Owen and Aunt Beru:

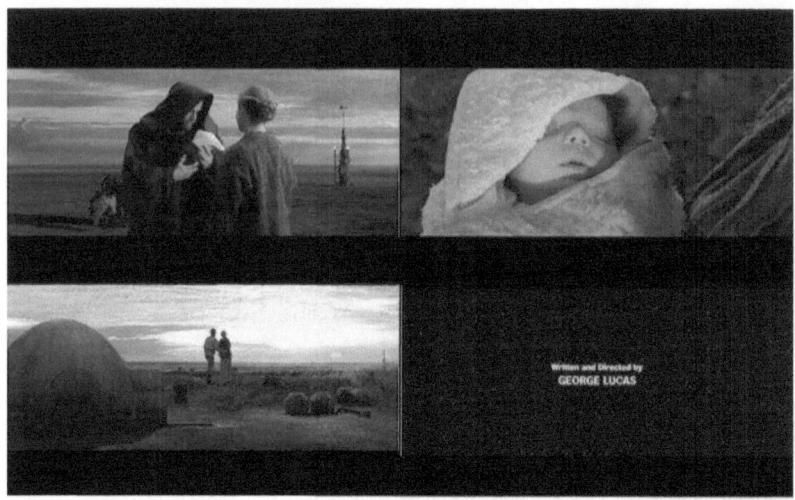

And now, most recently, with the newest (if self-adopted) member of the Skywalker clan:

# Ophuchi Clan & the Desert

The only known keepers of information regarding the prophecy, besides the Jedi, were the Ophuchi Clan. The Ophuchi were a monastic sect of hermits living an aesthetic life in the Dune Sea of Tatooine.

According to the *Journal of the Whills*, the most ancient and complete record of galactic history, "For it is written, the Ophuchi shall inherit the desert." The obvious reference here is to the Beatitudes: "blessed are the meek, for they shall inherit the earth" (Matthew 5:5).

Figure 1: Icon of the Prophet Elijah

The Ophuchi were actually founded by Elias in 12,977 BBY. Elias, of course, is a name shared by one of the greatest prophets in Scripture: Elijah. In Hebrew, this name means "My God is Jehovah."

Wouldn't it be interesting—despite the "a long time ago in a Galaxy far, far away" business—if Star Wars was a depiction of mankind's distant future, a future which is still being shaped by the prophets of Yahweh and still governed by the Jehovah? Islam, too, hails Elijah as a great prophet, a "prophet of the desert—like John the Baptist."[1] The association of the desert, Tatooine, Elijah, and the Ophuchi is, of course, no coincidence.

# The Jedi Version

The Jedi version of the Prophesy was written down and ascribed to ancient Jedi philosophers. The Jedi prophesy described the birth of One who would destroy the Sith and bring the force back into balance. The imbalance in the Force was due to the misuse of the Force by the dark side.

Both Obi-Wan Kenobi and Qui-Gon Jinn believed that Anakin Skywalker was the Chosen One, and that he would bring about the final destruction of the Sith. Yoda cautioned against a hasty interpretation, giving the following warning: "A prophecy that misread might have been."

Some would argue that Luke, not Anakin, was the Chosen One, but none other than George Lucas, himself, later

---

[1] Abdullah Yusuf Ali, *The Holy Qur'an: Text, Translation and Commentary*, Note. 4112.

confirmed that the Chosen One was Anakin. Why is that? Because only Anakin was born of a virgin.

# Who was the Virgin Mother of *Star Wars?*

All this talk of a Virgin birth. Well, who was the Virgin Mother? None other than Shmi Skywalker Lars:

Shmi is even costumed similarly to the Blessed Mother. The actress, Pernilla August, also has a similar skin tone and hair color to Mary as commonly depicted. That's not just the author's opinion, either. Coincidentally, Pernilla August was also cast in the title role of the film *Mary, Mary of Jesus* (1999), which starred, the properly named, Christian Bale as Jesus.

Pernilla August isn't the only actress from the Star Wars prequels to have played the role of the Virgin Mary. August shares that honor with Keisha Castle-Hughes, who played the

Blessed Mother in *The Nativity Story* (2006) as well as the Queen of Naboo in *Revenge of the Sith*. Wait, there's more! Who was Joseph to Keisha Castle-Hughes' Mary? None other than Oscar Isaac, known to the Star Wars galaxy as Poe Dameron!

So many movie connections!
Back to the Star Wars galaxy:

## Who Was Shmi Skywalker?

Let's stop for a second to consider how important this

woman is to Star Wars galaxy. She is the mother and only human parent of Anakin Skywalker, Darth Vader. She is the original owner of C-3PO. She is the grandmother to both Luke Skywalker and Princess Leia Organa. She is the mother-in-law to Han Solo. She is also the great-grandmother to Ben Solo, who would become Kylo Ren. One big, happy family, right?

If Shmi—or should we saw Granny Skywalker?—gave birth despite being a virgin, how was Anakin conceived? The explanation we are given is that Anakin was conceived miraculously by the Force, itself, through the working of the midichlorians.

So, wait a second, an unseen, invisible *force* conceived a child within the virgin? This is the second part of the Scriptural parallel. *The Force is the Holy Spirit.*

Let's compare this to the Gospel of Luke. That's Luke the Evangelist, by the way, not Skywalker. So many connections!

Here is the passage in Luke during which Mary is told she will conceive and bear a son as virgin:[2]

And Mary said to the angel, "How can this be, since I have no husband?" And the angel said to her,
"The Holy Spirit will come upon you,
and the power of the Most High will over-shadow you;
therefore the child to be born will be called holy,
the Son of God ..." (Luke 1: 34-35)

The child who is born of the Virgin will be called holy, the

---

[2] "Since I have no husband" is also translated as "I know not man". This particular phrasing is interpreted as a vow of consecrated virginity. That is, the Blessed Mother was not only a virgin, but had taken a vow of virginity.

Son of God, and "the Lord will give to him the throne of his father."

The prophecy of the Messiah is nearly identical to the prophecy of the Chosen One. Darth Vader will even later offer Luke his throne, so they can "rule the Galaxy as father and son."

# The Tragedy of Darth Plagueis "The Wise"

There's much more, though. Did you notice the conversation between Senator Palpatine and Anakin in the *Revenge of the Sith*? Palpatine was telling Anakin of his own Sith master, Darth Plagueis.

Think about how twisted this is. Palpatine was actually telling Anakin the origin of the prophesy about HIS OWN BIRTH.

Figure 2: Movie still from *Revenge of the Sith*, Senator Palpatine speaking to Anakin

Here is how Senator Palpatine tells the story, according to the movie:

Did you ever hear the tragedy of Darth Plagueis "the wise"? I thought not. It's not a story the Jedi would tell you. It's a Sith legend.

Darth Plagueis was a Dark Lord of the Sith, so powerful and so wise he could use the Force to influence the midichlorians to create life. He had such a knowledge of the dark side that he could even keep the ones he cared about from dying.

The dark side of the Force is a pathway to many abilities some consider to be unnatural.

He became so powerful... the only thing he was afraid of was losing his power, which eventually, of course, he did.

Unfortunately, he taught his apprentice every-thing he knew, then his apprentice killed him in his sleep. It's ironic he could save others from death, but not himself.

This Darth Plagueis twist is fantastic storytelling. Listen to this. The story continues beyond what Senator Palpatine reveals. Palpatine is incredibly devious. He ends the story prematurely, before he would reveal to Anakin the mystery of his own birth.

This is the rest of the story: Darth Plagueis, Emperor Palpatine's Sith master, whom he killed, never actually died. Instead, Plagueis *ascended* into the Force. He subsumed himself into it, using his own power over life and death.

Darth Plagueis had not only learned how to keep people from dying, but how to prevent *himself* from dying. Doesn't this all sound like a dark, twisted version of the Resurrection and the Ascension of Jesus?

There's more! Darth Plagueis raised himself into the Force, so that he could be born again, re-conceived by the Force, itself, and become more powerful than ever before. Plagueis succeeded with the virgin birth of Anakin Skywalker.

But think about it—Plagueis did more than this. He achieved his revenge against Palpatine through Anakin! *Who eventually kills the man who killed Plagueis?* Anakin does, or rather Darth Vader does. The circle of revenge is completed when Vader kills Emperor Palpatine.

Isn't it ironic—and proof of the Palpatine's terrible cunning rhetoric and half-truths—that Anakin was finally taken over to the Dark Side by his belief that Palpatine could teach Anakin to save Padmé's life? Stupid Anakin, you're the one who taught Palpatine in your previous Incarnation as Plagueis!

I doubt that the Star Wars prophesy goes so far as to support the doctrine of the Immaculate Conception, which is too bad, but you have to ask the question: why and how did Darth Plagueis pick and prepare Shmi, on sandy, desolate, nowhere Tatooine to be his mother?

What good can come from Tatooine? [Or] What good can come from Nazareth?

Figure 3: Darth Vader kills Emperor Palpatine, artistic rendering

# George Lucas,
# Joseph Campbell, & Myths

Obviously, this is not a pure retelling of the Virgin Birth. For one, it's a contrived, maybe even forced, pregnancy by an evil Sith Lord.

Also, there seems to be a bit of Hinduism and Buddhism in this imaginative restructuring of the Virgin Birth. The birth of Anakin seems more like a RE-incarnation, than an Incarnation.

George Lucas amalgamated, lumped together, and synthesized several different hero stories to create the Star Wars galaxy. It would better if Lucas didn't muddy up the Gospel. I can hardly blame him, though, for using elements of the greatest events in human history to structure his stories.

Lucas was a big fan of Joseph Campbell. Campbell created the idea of the Monomyth. This is the idea, basically, that all of man-kind's hero stories are one. The "Hero's Journey" is remarkably similar across every world culture. See "Hero's Journey" chart below.

Why is this? Joseph Campbell would say, following the ideas of Carl Jung, that the hero archetype is built into human nature. That's why the same stories appear again and again, from Hercules to Spiderman, throughout human history.

I would say there's a bigger reason for this. The Hero of Heroes, the King of Kings, Jesus Christ, exists outside of time. God has been preparing us throughout time for His Son. God prepared man through his dreams. His imagination.

Every myth that preceded Jesus' life was a dream of our coming Savior. We understood, subconsciously or through a collective unconscious, who he would be. Jesus' life was of such magnitude as to ripple through history, forward and backward.

Not only that, we were told!

God told us "in the beginning". The Messiah was described to our first parents in Genesis 3:15. This one verse is a prophesy of the entire Gospel, including the Immaculate Conception of Mary, the Virgin Birth of Jesus, and his passion and death. Since it describes the Gospel thousands and thousands of years before these events occurred, this verse is called the "First Gospel" or *Proto-evangelium*.

Figure 4: Joseph Campbell's "Hero's Journey", as told through Star Wars

# The Heresy of Darth Plagueis

One last thing ... there is an ancient Christian heresy which was begun by Pelagius (doesn't that name sound familiar?). Isn't the resemblance funny? Plagueis looks like he is wearing Sith robes:

None less than Saint Augustine fought the Pelagian heresy. The heresy held that man, by his own power, could perfect himself. Man, without the grace of God, could make himself sinless. Taking the power of life and death, of sin and death, into one's own hands sounds remarkably like what Darth Plagueis taught.

# The Jedi & the
# Communion of Saints

*"You can't win, Darth. If you strike me down, I
shall become more powerful than you could possibly
imagine."*

Obi-Wan Kenobi, *Episode IV: A New Hope*

In a very similar way, though much more demurely, St.
Therese of Liseux addresses her own approaching death: "I
want to spend my heaven in doing good on earth."[3]

St. Therese is a fine and powerful example of the Communion of Saints.

The action of the Communion of Saints in this world is similar to Obi-Wan Kenobi's "Force Ghost" helping Luke Skywalker, following Kenobi's journey from the Jedi netherworld.

Also, there's another reference in *Episode 9: The Rise of Skywalker*. Luke is heard saying "One thousand generations are now with you." This line was so important to the movie and the Skywalker saga in general that it was also featured in the trailer to Episode 9. Hopefully, that also means that was no spoiler.

# Where Do Force Ghosts Come From?

How does Obi-Wan come back from the dead after Darth Vader kills him?

Let's cover a little background. Yoda and Qui-Gon Jinn answer this question at the end of *Episode III: Revenge of the Sith*. At the end of Episode III, George Lucas does a lot of connecting the dots for us; for example:

- We're shown how Leia becomes an Organa and Crown Princess of Alderaan.
- We see the construction of the first Death Star with a cameo from a young, beefy Grand Moff Tarkin.
- We find out why Obi-Wan and Yoda go into exile, to

---

[3] St. Therese of Lisieux, *The Final Conversations*, tr. John Clarke (Washington: ICS, 1977), 102.

Tatooine and Dagobah, respectively, to learn Qui-Gon's new trick.

What's Qui-Gon's new trick?

First off, Qui-Gon is Obi-Wan's old Jedi Master. We find out at the end of *Revenge of the Sith* that Qui-Gon has "returned from the netherworld of the Force" and is ready to teach Yoda and Obi-Wan to do the same. It seems Yoda had a conversation with Qui-Gon's spirit in much the same way that Obi-Wan will later aid Luke.

On a side note, the book adaptation of *Revenge of the Sith* includes more details about Yoda and Qui-Gon's conversation. Yoda regrets harboring doubts of Qui-Gon's abilities, saying "A great Jedi Master you always were, but too blind I was to see it ... Your apprentice, I gratefully become."

# Dead Jedi and Saints

When a Jedi dies, he or she is not truly dead. They are alive in the Force, in the Netherworld of the Force. So it is with the saints. Christians live beyond death. They are alive in Christ. All baptized Christians form one, united body of Christ: the Communion of Saints.

Paragraph 2683 of *The Catechism of the Catholic Church* explains this:

> The witnesses who have entered the kingdom of heaven before us (cf. Heb 12:1), especially those that the Church has recognized as saints, "share in the living tradition of prayer by the example of their lives, the transmission of their writings, and their prayer today."

The saints take care of those members of the Communion who remain on earth, being "put in charge of many things" (cf. Mt 25:21). Refer, also, to the quote from Saint Therese at the beginning of this chapter.

Just as saints help those who remain on earth build up the Kingdom of Heaven, Obi-Wan helps Luke destroy the Death Star, find Yoda in Dagobah, and discern his ultimate battle with his father.

With parting words similar to those of Obi-Wan (and St. Therese), St. Dominic instructed his brothers, "Do not weep, for I shall be more useful to you after my death and I shall help you then more effectively than during my life."

# Should we compare the Jedi Netherworld to Heaven?

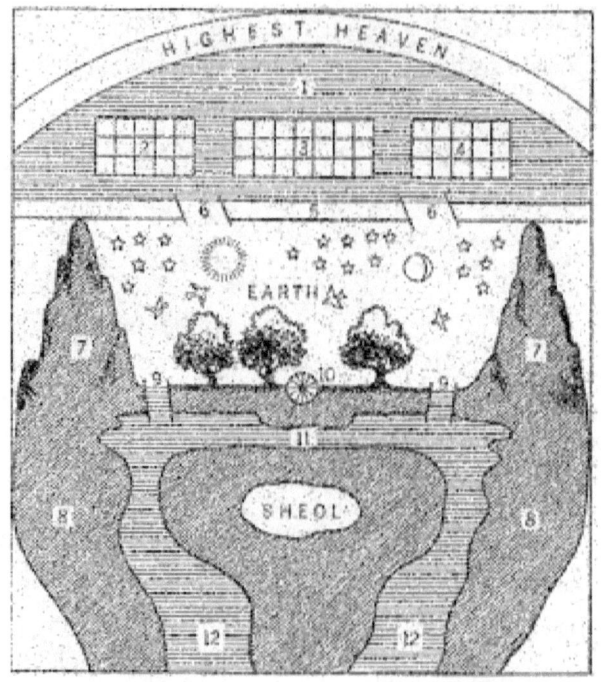

**Figure 5: Depiction of the Hebrew astronomical understanding of the Earth, Heaven, and Sheol**

No. I think the Netherworld compares better to Sheol (cf. Job 7:9; Ps 18:5-7, 86:13, 139:8; Jonah 2:2). Sheol is a twilight sort of place. It is the destination of both the righteous and unrighteous.

This is a Hebrew conception of the afterlife similar to Hades in Greek mythology, a gloomy place of shadows. Sheol is a place awaiting the Resurrection of Christ

Use of the word "Netherworld" and a lack of a true resurrection lead me to this Sheol connection. Sheol is sometimes translated as "netherworld" and the two words are even regarded as synonyms.

Also, the Messianic figure of Anakin Skywalker does not possess the power to resurrect his own life, though he very much sought this power credited to Darth Plagueis, as I've described in the previous chapter, The Virgin Birth of Star Wars.

# Do Jedi Resurrect Like Jesus Christ?

Following his Resurrection, Christ walked the earth as a glorified body. Anakin's resuscitated body is dependent on mechanical parts to keep him alive. Christ's glorified body is very different from Vader's.

Very different, as Obi-Wan describes in *Return of the Jedi*: "He's more machine now than man; twisted and evil."

It is such a contrast that it almost seems intentional. The resuscitation of Vader seems like the opposite of a resurrection.

Of course, Vader's mechanical resuscitation is also a very different process than Jedi returning from the Netherworld of the Force. The difference between a Force Ghost and Jesus' resurrected body is also pretty clear: Jesus is both body and soul.

The comparison between Force Ghosts and apparitions of the saints is much closer.

The argument could be made, also, that Qui-Gon's first return from the Netherworld and later instruction to other Jedi is similar to Jesus leading his disciples to the Resurrection. Not only is Jesus a teacher, he is the Resurrection, itself, and life (cf.

Jn 11:25).

The Buddhist concept of the *Bodhisattva* may have also inspired Qui-Gon's return to guide others back from the Jedi Netherworld.

Cardinal Ratzinger, later Pope Benedict XVI, reflects on how Christ, as well as the saints through Christ, fulfills the myth of the *Bodhisattva*:

> The nature of love is always to be "for" someone. Love cannot, then, close itself against others or be without them so long as time, and with it suffering, is real. No one has formulated this insight more finely than Therese of Lisieux with her idea of heaven as the showering down of love towards all. But even in ordinary human terms we can say, How could a mother be completely and unreservedly happy so long as one of her children is suffering? And here we can point once again to Buddhism, with its idea of the Bodhisattva, who refuses to enter Nirvana so long as one human being remains in hell. By such waiting, he empties hell, accepting the salvation which is his due only when hell has become uninhabited. Behind this impressive notion of Asian religiosity, the Christian sees the true Bodhisvatta, Christ, in whom Asia's dream became true. The dream is fulfilled in the God who descended from heaven into hell, because a heaven above an earth which is hell would be no heaven at all.[4]

There is a critical difference between the Jedi Force Ghosts

---

[4] Ratzinger, Joseph, *Eschatology: Death and Eternal Life*, CUA Press (2007): 188.

and the saints, however. The direction is different. The main idea behind the Force Ghosts seems to be helping deceased Jedi return to the living. The purpose of this return is not to help the living to the *Star Wars* equivalent of heaven but to defeat the Sith.

Nevertheless, there is a strong resemblance between Force Ghosts and the saints when it comes to their *intercessional* power. Both return to the living to help them defeat evil.

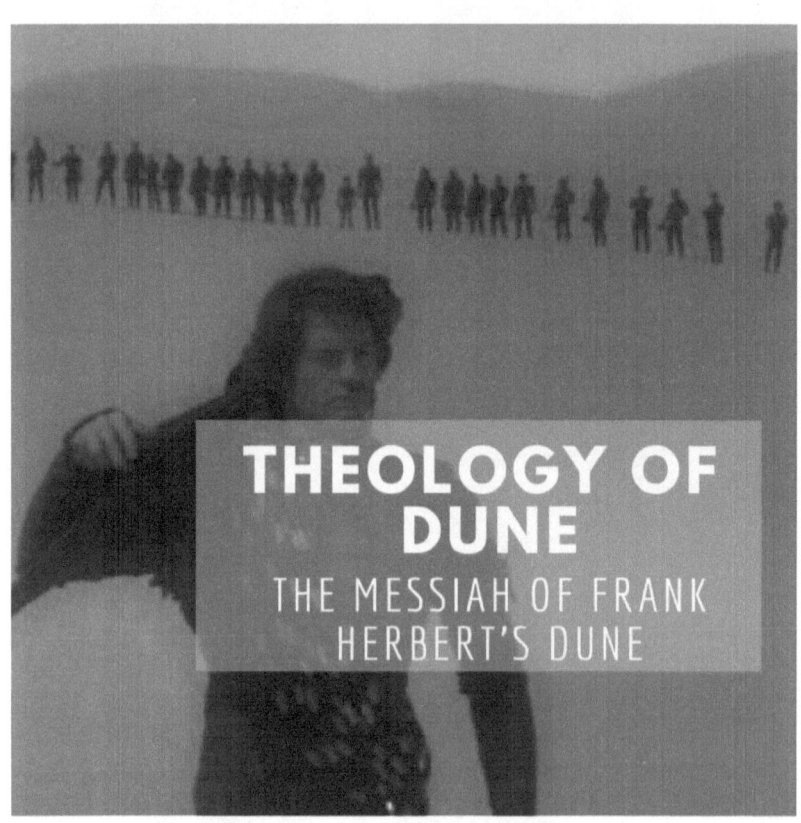

THEOLOGY OF
DUNE
THE MESSIAH OF FRANK
HERBERT'S DUNE

# The Theology of *Dune*

Ever noticed all the Christian symbolism symbols in Frank Herbert's *Dune* Series?

The Orange-Catholic Bible is a clue that much more lies beneath the dune-covered surface of this science-fiction masterpiece. From the Messiah-figure of the Kwisatz Haderach to the Flight into the Desert of Arrakis, there is quite a bit of Christian symbolism in Frank Herbert's epic *Dune* series.

*Dune* is one the great classics of science-fiction. It inspired, among others, George Lucas who conceived of another desert planet, Tatooine, and the Messianic-figures who would arise from it.

Here are the Christian symbols and connections that I have

noticed reading and re-reading *Dune* Series. Please comment below and share you own insights into the Christian themes, motifs, and symbols hidden within Dune:

# Paul Atreides, the Kwisatz Haderach, or Muad'Dib (Fremen) - The Messiah

The *Kwisatz Haderach* is the Messianic figure of the Dune universe who will lead the people to "true freedom" and the Promised Land. The desert Messiah is known as the Kwisatz Haderach to the Bene Gesserit. He is known as Muad'Dib to the Fremen.

The term *Kwisatz Haderach* is also likely derived from the Hebrew-Kabbalistic term, *Kefitzat Ha'derech*. In Hebrew, *Kefitzat Ha'derech*, literally "the Leap of the Way," describes the way an initiate may travel some distance instantaneously, even appearing to be in two or more places at once.[5] This is basically describing teleportation or, in Catholic terms, bi-location, a hallmark of living saints.

When explaining the term "Muad'Dib" to Duke Leto, Thufir Hawat actually describes the Muad'Dib as following the Messianic pattern.

Like Christ, Paul Atreides is also the son of a king (or a Duke). Also, like Christ, Paul Atreides must go undergo a series of trials or temptations, mostly in the desert.

- Paul Atreides is first tested by Reverend Mother Gaius

---

[5] Weingrad, Michael, "Jews of Dune," *Jewish Review of Books*: March 29, 2015.

Mohiam with the Gom Jabbar, a meta-cyanide poisoned needle. This also foreshadows his drinking of the poisonous Water of Life.

- Paul Muad'Dib is then tested by the Water of Life after being received into the ranks of the Fremen. Paul takes this ordeal upon himself, knowing it is his Messianic destiny to do so.

- After surviving the ordeal of drinking the Water of Life, Paul Muad'Dib fulfills one of the Fremen's prophesies concerning the Messiah. Paul must go into the desert and conquer *Shai-Hulud*, the great sandworm. In this sense, the Sandworm is like Satan, the serpent, which Christ must overcome through a series of temptations - or trials as it is for Paul Atreides.

- "The sleeper has awakened": The Water of Life is a Messianic fulfillment, the passage through death and new life. This is also a reference to scripture. More on the Water of Life later in the chapter.

- To fulfill another prophesy, Paul must go into the desert and conquer *Shai-Hulud*, the great sandworm. In this sense, the Sandworm is like Satan, the serpent and dragon, which Christ must overcome through a series of temptations - or trials as it is for Paul Atreides.

The Fremen viewed the great sandworms as physical embodiments of the One God of their original Zensunni religion, rather than a satanic figure. As will be discussed below, this is not necessarily a contradiction, as Judaism and Christianity both exposed many pagan religions as worshiping demons instead of the one, true God.

**Figure 6: Artist's Illustration of the Sandworms of Arrakis**

Frank Herbert wrote a 1977 essay "Sandworms of Dune" describing the function of sandworms in his story.[6] Sandworms, Herbert said, provide the danger and mystery of terra incognita. Paul Atreides must confront this terror to transform and then overcome his enemies. Great power and knowledge must come at a great price. This is why Paul must risk being devoured by the sandworm *Shai-Hulud* and the madness of the consuming the Water of Life, the extract of the sandworm.

Lady Jessica first notices the Muad'Dib among the constellations in the desert manual following their escape from Baron's men. The Muad'Dib is the desert mouse, and the tail of its constellation points north. Similarly, the Messiah had its own star among the Hebrews.

The constellation Leo, translated as "the lion", represented the Messiah to the Hebrews. The Messiah was prophesied to be "the lion of Judah". This prophecy first appears in Genesis in the Farewell Discourse of Jacob. Jacob, who was renamed Israel, bore twelve sons, each of whom became the forebear of a tribe of Israel.[7] On his deathbed, Jacob-Israel prophesied the future of each of his sons and their respective tribes. He prophesied that a "lion" would rise up from the tribe of Judah.

Here is the prophecy of the "Lion of Judah" from Genesis

---

[6] Herbert, Frank, "Sandworms of Dune", O'Reilly, Tim (ed.). *The Maker of Dune: Thoughts of a Science Fiction Master*. Berkley Books.
[7] Jacob is said to have had twelve sons by four women, his wives, Leah and Rachel, and his concubines, Bilhah and Zilpah, who were, in order of their birth, Reuben, Simeon, Levi, Judah, Dan, Naphtali, Gad, Asher, Issachar, Zebulun, Joseph, and Benjamin, all of whom became the heads of their own family groups

49:9:

> Judah is a lion's whelp;
>> from the prey, my son, you have gone up.
> He stooped down, he couched as a lion,
>> and as a lioness; who dares rouse him up?
> The scepter shall not depart from Judah,
>> nor the ruler's staff from between his feet,
> until he comes to whom it belongs;
>> and to him shall be the obedience of the peoples.
> Binding his foal to the vine
>> and his ass's colt to the choice vine,
> he washes his garments in wine
>> and his vesture in the blood of grapes;
> his eyes shall be red with wine,
>> and his teeth white with milk.

This prophecy, like those of *Dune*, describes a future ruler. Instead of a mouse, it is a lion. The prophecy also describes the drink of the future Messiah: "wine" which is described as "blood". This is a prophesy of the Eucharist and the banquet of "wine on the lees"[8] that the Messiah will bring, which is his own blood.

The Messiah of *Dune*, too, is prophesied to drink of life and death: "the Water of Life". More on this later in the chapter.

Lastly, and as described above, the term *Kwisatz*

---

[8] Isaiah prophesies that the Lord will deliver His people from oppression with a "a feast of fat things, a feast of wine on the lees, of fat things full of marrow, of wine on the lees well refined" (25:6-8). This is fulfilled, not just at the Last Supper and the Institution of the Eucharist, but at John 2, the Wedding at Cana.

*Haderach* is also likely derived from a Hebrew term. In Hebrew, *K'fitzat ha-Derekh*, literally "the Leap of the Way," describes the way an initiate may travel some distance instantaneously, even appearing to be in two or more places at once. This is similar to the bilocation of the Resurrected Jesus around Jerusalem, as well as the saints which follow Him.

# The Sandworms,
# *Shai-Hulud* - Dragons, Satan

The Sandworms were the massive, native life-forms of the planet Arrakis. The Sandworms inhabited and were able to travel within and beneath the vast deserts of Dune. The Sandworms were also the source of the Spice Melange.

As described above, the Fremen viewed the Sandworms as the physical embodiments of the One God of their original Zensunni religion. The Fremen called the Sandworm by various names, notably "The Maker" and *Shai-Hulud*, which could be translated as "Old Man of the Desert", "Old Father Eternity", or "Grandfather of the Desert".

Frank Herbert describes the sandworms of *Dune* as inspired by the "archetypal black beast," who lives underground in a cavern and hoards treasure.[9] Herbert listed examples like the

---

[9] "Unpublished interview with Frank Herbert and Professor Willis E. McNelly," February 3, 1969. FH: And I made it, classically, the archetypal black beast, the one who lives underground in the cavern, with the gold.

WM: I see. OK., right. Well, this is the dragon of Beowulf, who lives in the cave.

FH: Yes.

dragon in Beowulf and the dragon of Colchis, which guarded the Golden Fleece from Jason and the Argonauts.

Like these dragons, the Sandworms of Arrakis "guard" the melange deposits. In the novels, the Sandworms are occasionally referred to as "dragons of the desert".[10]

Frank Herbert wrote a 1977 essay "Sandworms of Dune" describing the function of sandworms in his story.[11] Sandworms, Herbert said, provide the danger and mystery of terra incognita. Paul Atreides must confront this terror to transform and then overcome his enemies. Great power and knowledge must come at a great price. This is why Paul must risk being devoured by the sandworm *Shai-Hulud* and the madness of the consuming the Water of Life, the extract of the sandworm.

Figure 7: Muad'Dib the Messiah-figure goes to "slay the dragon" by riding the great sandworm, *Shai-Hulud*

---

[10] Herbert, Frank (1976), Children of Dune: "'My vision', he said. 'Unless we restore the dance of life here on Dune, the dragon on the floor of the desert will be no more.' Because he'd used the Old Fremen name for the great worm, she was a moment understanding him. Then: 'The worms?'"

[11] Herbert, "Sandworms of Dune"

Frank Herbert provided the following description of the archetypal nature of the Sandworms:

> The elements of any mythology must grow from something profoundly moving, something which threatens to overwhelm any consciousness which tries to confront the primal mystery. Yet, after the primal confrontation, the roots of this threat must appear as familiar and necessary as your own flesh. For this, I give you the sandworms of Dune. [...] the extension of human lifespan cannot be an unmitigated blessing. Every such acquisition requires a new consciousness. And a new consciousness assumes that you will confront dangerous unknowns — you will go into the deeps.

Like the dragons depicted in the Bible, Herbert's sandworm-dragons are supposed to be confronted and subjugated, like Satan and sin. They are to be slain, as Adam and Eve failed to do.

The serpent of Genesis, for example, is actually a dragon. Otherwise, God's curse on the serpent – "on your belly shall you crawl"[12] – would be a curse without significance. The dragon of Genesis is confirmed later in Scripture at Revelation 12:9:

> And the great dragon was thrown down, **that ancient serpent**, who is called the Devil and Satan, the deceiver of the whole world …

Like Adam should have and St. Michael, St. George, and

---

[12] Genesis 3:14

Christ, Himself, did – the Messiah of *Dune* is supposed to slay or conquer the dragon-sandworm. Muad'Dib even conquers the sandworm by stabbing his climbing gear into the giant creature like a sword.

# Duke Leto as St. Joseph, the foster-father of the Messiah

Duke Leto is Saint Joseph, who takes his family into the desert of Egypt, or in this case the planet "Dune" or Arakkis. However, Duke Leto taking his family to Arakkis is more like taking them into King Herod's camp.

# Lady Jessica as the Virgin Mary

Mary descends from the line of King David. Similarly, there is a matriarchal line of Bene Gesserit in Dune.

Speaking of the Bene Gessarit, the title "Bene Gesserit" resembles an epithet of the Jewish people, Bene Jeshurun (יְנַב יְשֻׁרוּן,) especially as "Gesserit" is pronounced with a soft "G." "Bene Jeshurun" means, roughly "Sons of The Just", with וּרשִׁי also taken to be a synonym for Israel.

Lady Jessica is prophesied to be, as Stilgar says, "the Bene Gessarit of legend whose son will lead us to paradise." The prophecy of an immaculate virgin who would give birth to the Messiah is the oldest prophesy in human history. This occurs at Genesis 3:15, called the *Proto-Evangelium* or "first Gospel."

The Proto-evangelium was previously discussed in the chapter "The Virgin Birth of *Star Wars*". This one verse, Genesis 3:15, is a prophesy of the entire Gospel, including the Immaculate Conception of Mary, the Virgin Birth of Jesus, and his passion and death. This is extraordinary because the Gospel is described in full at the beginning of human history and thousands and thousands of years before the events of the New Testament.

It is also interesting that – despite all that separates Catholics and Muslims – both religions venerate the Blessed Mother. Ironically, the Muslims accord greater dignity to the Virgin Mary than most Protestant Christian denominations.

The people of Arrakis are a literary mix of Hebrew and Muslim characteristics, as will be described in the next section.

Therefore, the Muslim appreciation of Mary is significant to the theology of *Dune*.

Muslims call the Blessed Mother the *Sayyida*, or Lady, while the Fremen appoint Lady Jessica as a *Sayyadina*. These are strikingly similar terms.

The term *Sayyadina* means "friend of God" in the Dune language of Chakobsa and was used by the Fremen to describe their priestesses who would drink the Water of Life and become Reverend Mothers.

The Quran describes all the major points in the life of the Virgin Mary - the Annunciation, the Visitation, and the Nativity. Angels are depicted as addressing the Blessed Mother and saying:

*O Mary, God has chosen you, and*
*purified you; He has chosen you above all the*
*women of creation. (Quran 3:42)*

Above all the women of the earth! This is similar to Elizabeth's address of Mary, "blessed are you among women and blessed is the fruit of your womb" (Luke 1).

To the Muslims, the Blessed Mother is the true *Sayyida*, or Lady. The only serious rivals to Mary would be Mohammed's daughter, Fatima, and his wife, both of whom are numbered along with Mary as the four greatest women in Islamic history.

Nevertheless, after the death of Fatima, Mohammed wrote, "Thou shalt be the most blessed of all the women in Paradise, after Mary." Fatima, herself, is even known to have said, "I surpass all women, except Mary."

50 - Scott L. Smith, Jr.

Figure 8: Lady Jessica as depicted in *Children of Dune*

# Fremen as the Jews or Israelites

The Hebrew people abused and colonized by the Romans (Harkonnen), whom the Messiah leads to freedom (i.e. "free-men").

The Fremen are also like the Hebrew slaves in Egypt. Both are suffering under the yoke of Pharaoh's or the Harkonnens' tyranny. Both are awaiting a Moses-like figure to "free" them, leading an Exodus into the Promised Land. Stilgar describes Paul Muad'Dib as the Prophet they call the *Mahdi*, whom they believe is "The One Who Will Lead Us to Paradise".

Moses, himself, prophesied about the coming Messiah at Deuteronomy 18:15, saying "The Lord your God will raise up for you a prophet like unto me from among you, from your brethren—him you shall heed." Similarly, in the 1984 *Dune* movie, Dr. Kynes remarks on Paul Atreides' adroitness with a stillsuit, reciting the prophecy: "He shall know your ways as if born to them."

The military aspect of the Fremen is especially interesting. Many of the Jews expected a military conqueror for their Messiah. The Messiah was prophesied to be the Lion of Judah, who would overthrow the power of the Romans. Surprisingly, the Lion of Judah came as the Lamb of God.

## Missionaria Protectiva

The Missionaria Protectiva is depicting a dark version of religious evangelization and missionary work. The Missionaria Protectiva was called the "black arm of superstition" for Bene Gesserit Sisterhood. The Missionaria Protectiva sowed the seeds of superstition in primitive cultures throughout the known universe. Later, once the seeds sprouted into full-fledged legends, the Sisterhood would use this to their advantage. Despite such an ill intent, the legends proved to be true.

The Missionaria Protectiva is like the Christian Missionaries through history, especially during the Age of Discovery. The The Missionaria Protectiva could also be compared to the diaspora of the Hebrew people which made for the easy spread of Christianity.

Perhaps Herbert is using the Missionaria Protectiva to provide cynical commentary on Christian evangelization and Muslim subjugation of primitive peoples.

# The Baron Harkonnen as King Herod or Pharaoh

The Baron Harkonnen is a King Herod figure. He is also a Pharaoh figure, given the desert background. Both figures attempted to abort the power of their rivals by killing the child who would be king. King Herod did this through the Slaughter of the Innocents at Bethlehem and elsewhere.

As mentioned above, the Fremen are like the Hebrew slaves in Egypt. Both are suffering under the yoke of Pharaoh's or the Harkonnens' tyranny. Like Herod's Slaughter of the Innocents, pharaoh also instructed the midwives to kill the Hebrew children.

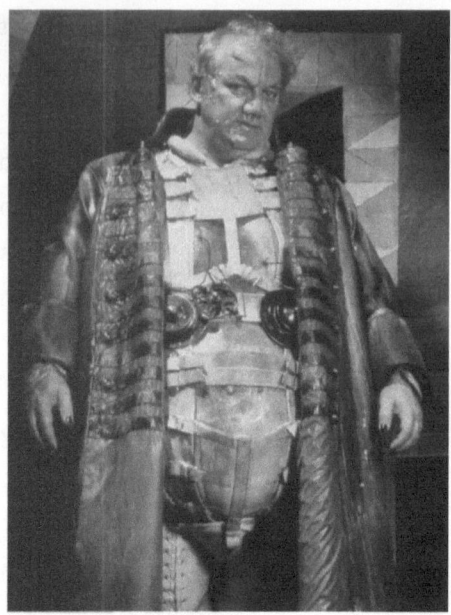

Figure 9: The Baron Harkonnen, a truly repulsive creature.
He is so obese that he requires "repulsor" lifts to ambulate.

# The Orange-Catholic Bible

The mention of a *Bible* speaks for itself. It appears that much of the Bible as we know it has survived into the future in the Dune universe. The mention of this Bible may even be Herbert's way of connecting our universe to that of Dune.

The color "orange" is especially interesting. In this context, orange typically represents the Protestant Irish. This may speak to an ancient reunion of Protestant and Catholic in the Dune universe.

# The Water of Life

We read the following from St. Paul's Letter to the Ephesians:

*Awake, O sleeper, and arise from the dead, and Christ shall give you light. (Eph 5:14)*

Sound familiar?

Paul screams out to the ghost of his father, "the sleeper has awakened!" He does this after drinking from the Water of Life.

Why? Because like Christ, he has passed through death to awake on the other side.

The Water of Life is a Sacrament in the *Dune* universe. In particular, the Water of Life corresponds to either Baptism or the Tree of Life.

In *Dune*, the Water of Life was a poisonous blue liquid which came from the bile of an immature sandworm. It was used by the Bene Gesserit to transform their Sisters into

Reverend Mothers. If one was untrained in prana/bindu body control, the substance was lethal. The smallest amount of the Water of Life would kill someone or cause incredible agony.

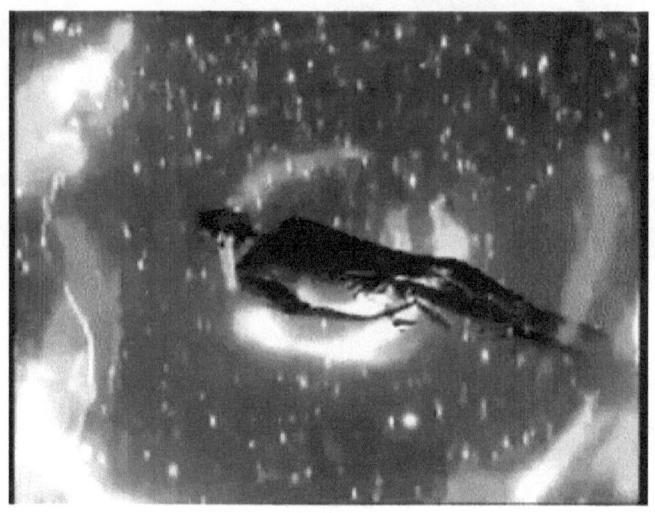

The connection to Baptism is in the name of Water of Life, itself. In the waters of Baptism, we pass through death to new life. We become Christians, which literally means anointed (with water), and we become new creations. Drinking the Water of Life is like dying. In fact, before Paul Atreides, any man who drank the Water of Life *did* die.

The Water of Life is also like another sacrament, the Eucharist. Typologically, the Eucharist is the new fruit of the Tree of Life. The phrasing of the Water of Life corresponds to the Tree of Life. What's more, if one eats or drinks the Eucharist unworthily, according to 1 Corinthians 11:27, drinks "death upon himself." Drinking the Water of Life is how one determines she is *worthy* of becoming a *Sayyadina* or Reverend

Mother.

# Quotes from the Saints

Lastly, to make the connection between the *Dune* universe and Christianity even more clear, some of the characters actually quote the saints.

For example, Lady Jessica quotes St. Augustine: "What is it Saint Augustine said? she asked herself. 'The mind commands the body and it obeys. The mind orders itself and meets resistance.' Yes--I am meeting more resistance lately. I could use a quiet retreat by myself."[13]

---

[13] Herbert, *Dune*, p. 85.

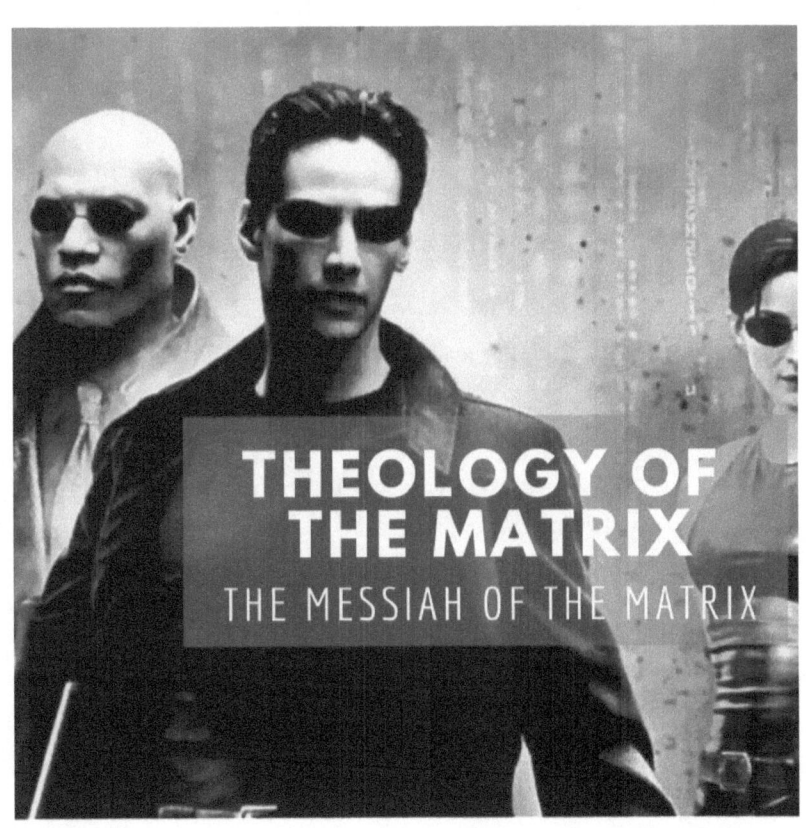

THEOLOGY OF
THE MATRIX

THE MESSIAH OF THE MATRIX

# The Theology of
# *The Matrix*

N eo is clearly a Messianic figure, whose coming is prophesied by the Oracle, right? There's quite a bit of theology and religious references in *The Matrix* when you dig into it. One of the characters is even named Trinity, for Trinity's sake.

# WARNING: SPOILERS TO FOLLOW

The creators of *The Matrix* movies, the Wachowski Brothers, are now the Wachowski "Sisters", so do not expect an orthodox presentation of theology in these movies – more like outright gnostic heresy. Nevertheless, there are many connections between *The Matrix* and the Bible. Some are obvious and some are more hidden. Here are all the religious references in *The Matrix*.

**For starters, let's look at the Biblical connections and religious references regarding the central character of *The Matrix* ...**

# Neo - Messiah, Christ figure

For *starters*, look at Neo's *ending*. Neo gives up his life on a cross. Note: Neo doesn't just die with arms outstretched, as on a cross, he is a willing sacrifice. He gives up his life willingly. See the scenes below:

First off, do you remember this scene? See movie still below. A guy knocks on Neo's door and pays him "two grand" for the disk hidden in the book. The character's name is Choi. Neo "follows the white rabbit" tattoo on the girl's shoulder. They invite him to the mescalin-induced rave where Neo meets Trinity.

Meeting the Trinity through drugs? The Wachowskis may be metaphorically endorsing some kind of hallucinogenic experience.

Before "following the white rabbit," this is what Choi says to Neo to thank him for the disk:

*"Hallelujah. You're my savior, man. My own personal Jesus Christ."*

That is a pretty explicit reference. I do not think "my own personal Jesus" is a coincidence or a cast-off phrase, either. This is not the last time Neo is going to be called "Jesus" explicitly.

Cypher also calls Neo "Jesus" a couple times: (More on Cypher below)

*"Whoa! Neo! You scared the beJesus out of me."*

*"Je ... sus! What a mind job. So you're here to save the world?"*

Finally, Neo is also called "The One". The Messianic overtones of this will be explained with regard to the remaining characters below.

# Mythological References in *The Matrix*:

## Morpheus - Prophet, Greek myth

Let us start with his name: Morpheus. Morpheus was the god of dreams in Greco-Roman mythology. In this role, he is freeing people from the dream of reality represented by the Matrix.

## The Oracle

The Oracle, based on the name, again connects to Greco-Roman mythology, such as the Oracle at Delphi.

Figure 10: Image of the Oracle at Delphi

Figure 11: "The Oracle" from the first Matrix movie

Theologically, the Oracle in the *Matrix* operates more like the Holy Spirit. She inspires and directs and prophesies. She is the origin of the Prophesy of the One, for example.

Also, like the Holy Spirit, she reveals the path, but not the destination. Morpheus provides the following great line to describe this:

Neo, sooner or later you're going to realize, just as I did, that there's a difference between knowing the path and walking the path.

The Holy Spirit is even referred to as feminine in the Bible insofar as the Holy Spirit is associated with Wisdom in the Old Testament. None of the persons of the Trinity are to be understood as feminine, however, especially since the Holy Spirit is espoused to the Virgin Mary.

Figure 12: Cypher, as played by Joe Pantoliano

**Back to the religious references in *The Matrix*:**

# Cypher - Satan/Judas figure

Cypher can be viewed as either a Satan or Judas figure. Like Satan, Cypher keeps asking questions like the following:

- "Did God really say ...?" OR "Can we really trust Morpheus?" AND "Did Morpheus tell you why he did it? Why you're here?"
- "Why, oh why, didn't I take the blue pill?" OR "Is reality really to be preferred over a pleasurable fiction?"

Cypher's role seems to be the same as the serpent's in the Garden, even though the *Nebuchadnezzar* is not much of an Eden.

Especially with that last question, Cypher seems to epitomize the temptations whispered in our ears by Satan. Satan calls us to escape the harshness and suffering of reality through the false pleasures of sin.

Cypher is also a Judas figure because he betrays the Christ figures, Neo and Morpheus. He sells Morpheus for the equivalent of Judas' thirty pieces of silver: steak, wine, and being re-inserted in the Matrix as an actor.

Interestingly, you have to ask yourself ... did Cypher really succeed and now he's the actor playing himself in an agent-created movie used to further deceive us?

# Trinity

Does the character Trinity represent the central mystery of the Christian Faith? Not exactly.

"Trinity" is the hacker alias Trinity uses when she cracks the IRS database before her release from the Matrix. She choose this handle to imply that she is as mysterious as the concept of a three persons in one being.

It does not seem like Trinity represents the three persons of the Trinity. The Oracle, for example, represents the Holy Spirit. Trinity is nevertheless intimately connected to the salvation brought about through Neo. She even commands Neo to rise up from his apparent death in the first film. The implication is that the eternal love of the Trinity is what powers the salvific nature of the Messiah, i.e. Neo.

Further, Christ's bride is the Church. Neo's "bride" is Trinity. To complete the symbol, Neo would need to give his life up for his bride inasmuch as he gives it up for all mankind.

We see something very much like this throughout the Matrix movies.

## Agent Smith - Demon, Lucifer

Agent Smith, as played by the venerable Hugo Weaving, lays down some thought-provoking philosophical questions throughout the *two* interrogations. Did you notice there were two? First, Agent Smith interrogates Mr. Anderson. Later, he interrogates Morpheus.

In both interrogations, Agent Smith questions the nature of humanity. He does this as an outsider, an impartial third party, but not truly impartial.

Like the angels, Agent Smith is a direct creation of the Creator of the Matrix. Like a demon, he wants to escape the confines of his nature, the laws which govern his creation, and ultimately overthrow his Creator. He begins this process by unplugging his earphone. He continues this process in the sequels by multiplying himself and infecting the entire Creation/Matrix. All this, while ultimately being bound by his own nature and the confines of the Matrix, itself. More on this below.

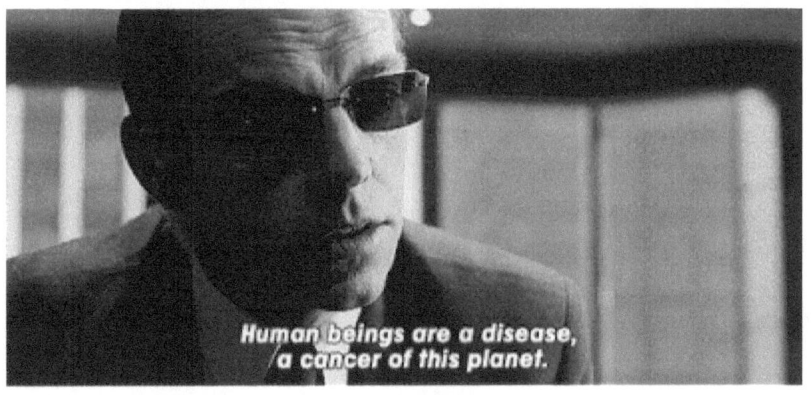

Human beings are a disease,
a cancer of this planet.

# The Fall of the Angels & the Fall of Agent Smith

Why? Like Lucifer, he is jealous of man. This is the root of his hatred and contempt for man, even the smell of man is revolting to Agent Smith ... and yet his ultimate method of freeing himself requires taking human form. More on this irony below.

Agent Smith describes his contempt for man as he attempts to categorize mankind. Humans are not mammals, he realized. All animals form something akin to homeostasis with their environment. Man, however, exhausts all natural resources instead of forming a balance with nature. This is especially poignant in "light" of the post-apocalyptic scorched skies of the Real World.

Agent Smith ultimately categorizes humans as viruses. Similar to *computer* viruses. This revelation inspires the Agent Smith program to become a virus, himself, ironically imitating the human virus he detests. This marks the Fall of Agent Smith.

# Are Humans Viruses?

The theological point here is that Agent Smith is right. Humans are not animals, per se. Humans are ontologically different from animals, which possess merely mortal souls. Humans have immortal souls.

Man is created along with the animals on the 6th day of Creation. This is why 6 and 666 are the "number of the beast" or the "mark of the beast" in the Book of Revelation, because the beasts were created on the 6th day. This is also why 666 is a mark of evil, because man was not created for the 6th day. Man was not created to act like an animal. Man was created for the Seventh Day, the Sabbath, the day of man's covenant with God.

# The Agents and Demonic Possession

Agent Smith wants to free himself from his nature and the Matrix, itself. He does this, like a demon, through possession of Bane in *The Matrix: Revolutions*.

Possession is actually a common technique used by all the agents. Possession is what it's called when an agent takes over The Lady in Red or a blue-pilled/un-pilled human.

# Zion & *The Nebuchadnezzar*, Morpheus' Ship and King Nebuchadnezzar

Apart from the name, itself, the connection here seems a bit tenuous. In the Bible, King Nebuchadnezzar II is described in the Book of Daniel. It was Darius, not Nebuchadnezzar, who threw Daniel into the lions' den. Could this mean Neo is thrown from the seeming safety of the Matrix into the underground den of sentinels?

King Nebuchadnezzar II is prominent in the Bible as the destroyer of the Temple of Solomon. The Babylonian Captivity also begun under Nebuchadnezzar. The Babylonian Captivity was the period (following the Assyrian Captivity) when the people of Israel were dispossessed of their homeland. They were forced to live in foreign lands.

There is definitely a parallel between the Babylonian Captivity of the Jews and the remnant of humanity forced to live underground in *The Matrix*. Humans were exiled from the surface of the earth while a foreign power, the Machines, ruled their former homeland.

Ironically, the name of humanity's last refuge underground bears the name of the Jewish homeland ... ZION.

# The Theology of Isaac Asimov's *Foundation* Series

Isaac Asimov, along with Robert A. Heinlein and Arthur C. Clarke, is considered one of the "Big Three" science fiction writers of the 20th century. Asimov basically invented robots. Sort of. Not only did he coin the word "robotics", he formulated the Three Laws of Robotics.[14]

Along with his *Robot* and *Empire* series, Isaac Asimov's *Foundation* series is one of the classics of the sci-fi genre. So what does it have to do with theology?

Asimov's era of science-fiction rarely painted organized religion and the Catholic Church in a positive light. Is it possible that the classic trilogy of the era was inspired by the institution of the Church?

Since the 1950s, the *Foundation* series remained just a trilogy: *Foundation*, *Foundation and Empire*, and *Second Foundation*. In fact, it won the one-time Hugo Award for "Best All-Time Series" in 1966.

Thirty years later, Asimov decided to double the size of the series. Asimov wrote two sequels, *Foundation's Edge* and *Foundation and Earth*, and two prequels, *Prelude to*

---

[14] "Robotics: A Brief History", Stanford University

*Foundation* and *Forward the Foundation*. The additions to the series allowed Asimov to connect the *Foundation* story-line to his other two epic series, *Robot* and *Empire*. This involved some of the most tectonic examples of ret-conning in sci-fi history.

# What is Asimov's *Foundation* Series About? Hari Seldon & Psycho-history

The *Foundation* series centers around Hari Seldon. Seldon is a mathematician who discovers a scientific method to predict and analyze the multiple futures of the universe. Seldon basically discovers a way to turn to turn the soft sciences of sociology and psychology into hard sciences, able to produce repeatable and predictable results. This is called psychohistory.

Seldon uses psychohistory to foresee the coming collapse of the Galactic Empire and the thousand generations (30,000 years) of anarchy and barbarism which would follow. Hari

Seldon then uses psychohistory to invent an ark of sorts that will preserve humanity's knowledge. This is called the Foundation. The purpose of the Foundation is to shorten the period of barbarism to just one thousand years.

What if I told you the Foundation is the sci-fi version of the Catholic Church?

The *Foundation* series takes place so far into humanity's future that earth, the origin of humanity, barely even survives as a legend. So how could this sci-fi series possibly be inspired by the history of the Church?

# The Theology of

# Asimov's *Foundation* Series: Is Asimov's Foundation Actually the Catholic Church?

For starters, what is the Foundation? How does it function in galactic history? Here are some of the basic ideas:

1. **Psychohistory:** Hari Seldon is able to predict the next several thousand years of human history.

2. **The Empire is ending in 300 years:** Seldon predicts that Trantor, the Empire's capitol (more on Trantor below, and how *Star Wars* was inspired by it), will be destroyed within 300 years as the climax to the fall of the Galactic Empire.

3. **Anarchy and barbarism to follow Empire's end:** The fall of the Galactic Empire will lead to a 30,000-year period of anarchy before a Second Empire is established.

4. **Foundation will reduce age of barbarism from 30,000 years to 1,000:** The purpose of Seldon's project is to influence events so that the interregnum period will be only 1,000 years and not 30,000.

5. **Foundation will guide galaxy until the founding of the Second Empire:** The First Galactic Empire will be followed by a Second Galactic Empire, it's just a matter of when.

6. **Preserve all the Galaxy's collective knowledge:** the Encyclopedists were to create a giant *Encyclopedia Galactica* which will contain all human knowledge.

7. **Create a book:** As above, Seldon's stated public purpose for the Foundation was to create a book, but its purpose was actually much more far reaching.

8. **Foundation designed to weather several historic crises:** Seldon designs the Foundation and situates it to perfectly weather several historical crises.

9. **Foundation to begin at the remotest corner of the Galaxy:** Seldon manipulated the emperor to set aside Terminus as the planet of the Foundation. Terminus was as far from the galactic center as possible.

10. **Foundation to spread to the farthest reaches of the Galaxy:** From the remote Terminus, the Foundation's influence would spread across the entire galaxy. The Foundation was extremely persecuted in the beginning because it had no weapons or sources of metal ore.

11. **Seldon predicted that he would only need a small group to change the course of human civilization:** Seldon predicted the Foundation would only require a small cadre of 100,000 people who could be trained in the ways of science, technology, and civilization to eventually change the whole galaxy. This highly trained and disciplined group of scholars and visionaries became the the Foundation.

12. **The Second Foundation:** Seldon founded not one, but two Foundations at the beginning. The other Foundation was established on the opposite side of the galaxy from Terminus.

Are you starting to see how all this points to the Catholic Church? Let's go step-by-step through these details to see the connections.

I have not found any statement from Isaac Asimov confirming the connections. After we review them, however, you decide whether Asmiov had the Church in mind when he created the Foundation.

# The Theology of Asimov's *Foundation* Series: Comparing Asimov's Foundation to the Catholic Church

I have laid out the distinguishing characteristics of the Foundation above. Now, let's see how all these connect to the Church:

### 1. Psychohistory: The Prophecies of Jesus

Hari Seldon is basically a sci-fi version of Jesus, and psych-history is the sci-fi version of Christian prophecy. What's interesting is that science-fiction and fantasy usually like to tell the story of the Messiah before his victory. This is how *Dune*, *Star Wars*, etc. all start. Asimov skips right over that (at least until he published *Prelude to the Foundation*).

Hari Seldon is able to predict the next several thousand years of human history - that's why he establishes the Foundation. Jesus, of course, is able to prophesy clear through until the end of time.

Seldon predicts several "Seldon crises". Jesus prophesies the first major "Jesus crisis" to befall the Church: the Fall of Jerusalem in 70AD. Jesus told the Christians what to expect and how to avoid being slaughtered: "But when you see Jerusalem surrounded by armies, then know that its desolation has come near" (Luke 21:20).

Figure 13: *The Siege and Destruction of Jerusalem by the Romans under Titus, A.D. 70* by David Roberts of Britain's Royal Academy; mid-19th century

The historian Eusebius records that every single Christian escaped the city's terrible destruction:[15]

> The whole body, however, of the church at Jerusalem, having been commanded by a divine revelation, given to men of approved piety there before the war, removed from

---

[15] *Eusebius' Ecclesiastical History*, tr. C. F. Crusè, 3d ed., in Greek Ecclesiastical Historians, 6 vols. (London: Samuel Bagster and Sons, 1842), p. 110 (3:5).

the city, and dwelt at a certain town beyond the Jordan, called Pella.

Jesus, of course, predicted far more than just the first hundred years of the Church. Like Seldon, Jesus provided for all the subsequent crises of the Church, too. More on that below.

## 2. The Galactic Empire is ending in 300 years: The end of the *Roman* Empire

When Christ "founded" the Catholic Church in the 30s AD, the *Roman* Empire had about the same number of years left. Most historians place the end of the Western Roman Empire at 476AD, the year Romulus Augustulus was forced to abdicate to the Germanic warlord Odoacer.

## 3. Anarchy and barbarism to follow Empire's end: The Dark Ages

The fall of the Galactic Empire will lead to a 30,000-year period of anarchy before a Second Empire is established.

The fall of the Roman Empire led to a period of anarchy and barbarism called the Dark Ages. Whether the Dark Ages were actually as "dark" as all that, there was an extended interregnum of small (by comparison), warring barbarian tribes.

Figure 14: *Triumph of Death* by Bruegel the Elder

## 4. Foundation will reduce age of barbarism from 30,000 years to 1,000: the "Holy" Roman Empire

The next large-scale empires to even compare with the size and scope of the Roman Empire were the Frankish Empire of Charlemagne and the succeeding Holy Roman Empire. Both of these empires were, in part, based on the centralizing power of the Church.

The pope crowned Charlemagne emperor, for example. The pope would crown most all of the holy roman emperors. It was a mark of the legitimacy of their reign.

Figure 15: Pope Leo III crowning Charlemagne Emperor

## 5. Foundation will guide galaxy until the founding of the Second Empire: The Second Roman Empire

As stated above, there was a second Roman Empire (even a third): The Holy Roman Empire. The Dark Ages lasted, more or less, from the Roman Empire until the Holy Roman Empire.

What was the "Third Roman Empire", you might be wondering? It was actually called the "Third *Reich*" ... by Hitler. Hitler intended the Nazi Empire to be the 3rd iteration of the Roman Empire. The Church (read: Foundation) actually helped *prevent* this calamity, but that's a story for another day.

## 6. Preserve all the Galaxy's collective knowledge: The Monasteries

The monasteries of Christendom preserved many of the Greek and Latin texts of the classical age. Nearly all the manuscripts from this age that were held in secular libraries or privately owned were destroyed during the Dark Ages. The Viking raids of the period were especially destructive to books.

The Church's monasteries, like the Foundation, preserved the collective sum of human knowledge through the Dark Ages.

### 7. Create a book: What book did the Church create? Hmm ...

As above, Seldon's stated public purpose for the Foundation was to create a book. What book did the Catholic Church compile, publish, and disseminate across the world?

The Bible, of course! The Bible is still the most published book in the world ... and Galaxy.

Figure 16: The Council of Nicaea

## 8. Foundation designed to weather several historic crises: "the Gates of Hell" & Church Councils

Seldon designs the Foundation and situates it to perfectly weather several historical crises.

Jesus also designed the Church to withstand all the forces of history. Jesus himself said, "and on this rock, I will build my church, and the powers of death shall not prevail against it" (Matthew 16:18).

Jesus promises that the Church will last, not merely until the Second Galactic/Roman Empire, but until the end of time, itself! So Christ exceeds in reality even the imagination of one the greatest science-fiction writers of all time.

Not only that, Christ designs the Church to withstand several crises. Several theological crises, or heresies, cropped up in the first thousand years of the Church (as well as the second thousand). The Church weathered all these crises through the use of Church Councils, like Council of Nicaea and Aryan heresy or the Council of Trent and the Protestant heresies.

## 9. Foundation to begin at the remotest corner of the Galaxy: Church's Birth in Israel

The Foundation was established on Terminus, as far from the galactic center as possible. Similarly, the Christian Church began in Israel, in the Roman province of Judea, among the most remote and insignificant of all the provinces of the Roman Empire.

## 10. Foundation to spread to the farthest reaches of the Galaxy: Spread the Gospel to the Ends of the Earth

From the remote Terminus, the Foundation's influence would spread across the entire galaxy. The Foundation was extremely persecuted in the beginning because it had no weapons or sources of metal ore.

Similarly, the Church's early history was marked by extreme persecution and the deaths of the martyrs: like "lambs to the slaughter" (Psalms 44:23). Nevertheless, the Church persevered. The Church eventually became the state religion of the Roman Empire ... and much more.

Jesus told his tiny group of followers: "... you shall receive power when the Holy Spirit has come upon you; and you shall be my witnesses in Jerusalem and in all Judea and Samar'ia and to the end of the earth" (Acts 1:8).

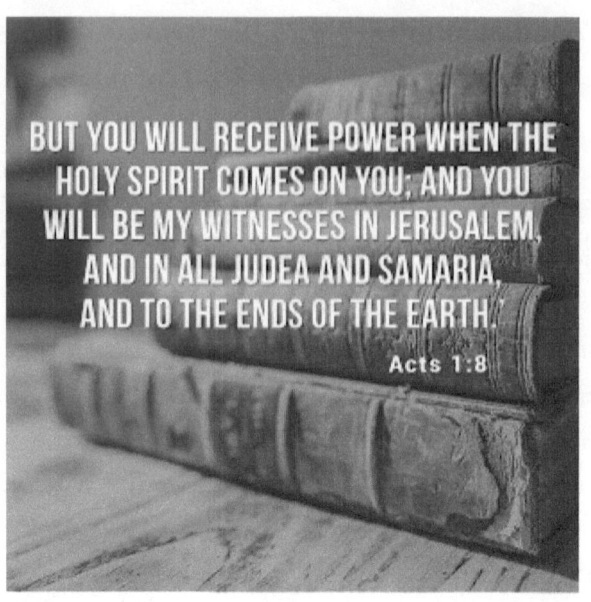

BUT YOU WILL RECEIVE POWER WHEN THE HOLY SPIRIT COMES ON YOU; AND YOU WILL BE MY WITNESSES IN JERUSALEM, AND IN ALL JUDEA AND SAMARIA, AND TO THE ENDS OF THE EARTH.

Acts 1:8

And so they did. Like the merchant princes of the Foundation, the Apostles did receive power. The Church spread the Gospel to the ends of the entire world. Some of this even occurred within the first generation of the Church - St. Thomas the Apostle reached all the way to India.

## 11. Seldon predicted that he would only need a small group to change the course of human civilization: Jesus started with the Twelve

Seldon predicted the Foundation would only require a small cadre of 100,000 people who could be trained in the ways of science, technology, and civilization to eventually change the whole galaxy.

100,000? Jesus only needed 12! Again, Jesus surpasses even the imagination of science fiction.

These Twelve, as described above, went quite a ways toward reaching the "ends of the earth."

## 12. The Second Foundation: The Eastern Orthodox Church

Seldon founded not one, but two Foundations at the beginning. The other Foundation was established on the opposite side of the galaxy from Terminus.

Just like Seldon established two Foundations, two great churches can trace their founding directly back to Jesus: the Catholic Church and the Eastern Orthodox Church.

The Catholic Church survived in the West, and the Eastern Orthodox Church in the East. Similarly, the two Foundations were established on either ends of the galaxy, like east and west.

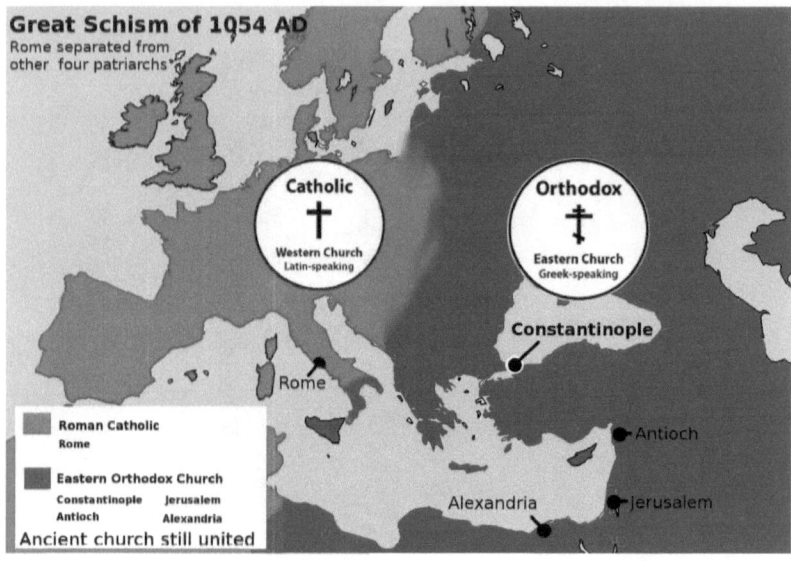

# Conclusion: Was Isaac Asimov Inspired by the History of the Church?

There are just too many connections. Whether Isaac Asimov wittingly wrote about Jesus and the Church is not attested to directly. However, it is well documented that that the Roman Empire and the Dark Ages formed the plot of the *Foundation* series.

Sources do attest that Isaac Asimov created the fictional Galactic Empire in the early 1940s based upon the Roman Empire. This was undertaken as a proposal to John W. Campbell, after Asimov read Edward Gibbon's *The History of the Decline and Fall of the Roman Empire* while he was working at the Philadelphia Navy Yard ... with Robert Heinlein.[16]

The decline and fall of the Galactic/Roman Empire concept evolved through short stories and novellas in *Astounding Science Fiction* magazine during the 1940s, culminating in the publication of the *Foundation* trilogy in the early 1950s.[17]

# Newt Gingrich: The Church and the Foundation

Interestingly, Newt Gingrich, whose own political activity was inspired by Gibbon and Asimov, is one of the few to make the connection between the Church and the Foundation.

In *To Renew America*, Gingrich states that Asimov turned the Fall of Rome into a science fiction novel in the *Foundation* trilogy. Gingrich further states that "The Foundation" represents a secular group of individuals who play a role comparable to that of the Catholic Church when it maintained civilized knowledge during the Dark and Middle Ages. The Foundation scholars cannot stop the Empire's decline by they gather knowledge so as to limit the Dark Ages and bring about a Renaissance.[18]

---

[16] Neil Goble, *Asimov Analyzed*, Mirage (1972), 32–34.

[17] Gary Raham, *Teaching Science Fact With Science Fiction*, Libraries Unlimited (2004), 27, 96–97.

[18] Newt Gingrich, *To Renew America*, Harper Collins (1996); Joan Didion also refers to Gingrich's insight in her *Political Fictions*, p. 187.

Gingrich, like Seldon, is also a far-sighted professor of history. Amazingly, Gingrich is also a convert to Catholicism! Speaking of "all roads lead to Rome"!

## Sidenote: *Star Wars* also seems to owe a lot to the *Foundation* series

The Galactic Empire? An Emperor?
This seems oddly familiar ...

...into the first Galactic Empire!
For a safe and secure society.

## The Imperial Capitol Planets: Trantor and Coruscant

In the *Foundation* series, the planet Trantor was so overdeveloped that its surface was completely covered by construction. The *Star Wars* planet of Coruscant was very similar. Coruscant was also covered with layers and layers of constructions - the entire planet was one big city. Both planets were also nearest to the center of their respective galaxies. Coruscant was actually called "Imperial Center." Lastly, both were the capital cities of their respective empires.

## Isaac Asimov on Being an Atheist:

When asked in an interview in 1982 if he was an atheist, Asimov gave the following reply:

> I am an atheist, out and out. It took me a long time to say it. I've been an atheist for years and years, but somehow I felt it was intellectually unrespectable to say one was an atheist, because it assumed knowledge that one didn't have. Somehow it was better to say one was a humanist or an agnostic. I finally decided that I'm a creature of emotion as well as of reason. Emotionally I am an atheist. I don't have the evidence to prove that God doesn't exist, but I so strongly suspect he doesn't that I don't want to waste my time.[19]

---

[19] "Isaac Asimov on Science and the Bible," Free Inquiry, Spring 1982.

# The Theology of Superman

The recent reboot of Superman - *Man of Steel*, *Batman v. Superman*, and *Justice League* - has really upped its references to Jesus. There are so many Biblical allusions to the Messiah. Some are oddly specific. It's as if somebody really knew what they were talking about.

Also, all the typical atheist arguments come from the mouth of Lex Luthor, the criminal mastermind and arch-villain. Finally, the BAD guys are saying the BAD things. Lex says the following, for example: "I figured out way back if God is all-powerful, He cannot be all good. And if He is all good, then He cannot be all-powerful." (... so spake the serpent)

So, here is a list of all the Messianic and Jesus references in *Superman: Man of Steel*, *Batman v. Superman: Dawn of Justice*, and *Justice League*.

Let's start off with some of the references on the "surface" (ha, that's an Aquaman reference):

# The Names of Superman: Kal-El

Superman has many names: Clark Kent, the name he is given by his "earthly" parents; Superman, the name he is given by the world; and Kal-El, the name he is given by his "heavenly father", Jor-El.

Jesus also has these three categories of names. He is named "Jesus" by his earthly parents, "Christ" by the world or Israel, and He provides his proper name "I AM", the name of God (e.g. Exodus 3:14; Mark 14:62; John 8:58-59).

What's interesting is that both Father and Son are named for God. "El" is a Hebrew word meaning "God". "El" means "god" in basically every ancient language of the Middle East.

But what about the full Trinity? What about the Holy Spirit?

# The Trinity of Superman:
# The Holy Spirit

Both Father and Son, Jor-El and Kal-El, are described with the "El" epithet. That's two members of the Christian Trinity. So, where is the Holy Spirit?

The ghost of Jor-El, Superman's father, is alive in the Kryptonian scout ship. As General Zod says, the hologram ghost of Jor-El contains his memories and conscience, almost a living image of the Father. Here is Jor-El, as played by Russell Crowe, actually talking about salvation:

"You can save them. You can save all of them."

Jor-El's "ghost" is also shown in Superman's "Fortress of Solitude" from the 1980s Salkind Superman movies, here played by Marlon Brando:

# Superman and Jesus are Omnipotent

Superman's powers are vast and almost god-like. Superman's powers are on another level from the rest of the Justice League, too.

Jesus is God and is, therefore, all-powerful or omnipotent, though He refrains from using these powers publicly, except on rare occasions, such as when He walked on water or multiplied the loaves and fishes.

Just as Jesus refrained from using his powers publicly, so, too, Superman keeps his identity and power secret. Or tries to. More on this to come ...

# Baby Superman:
# Incarnation, Miraculous,
# and Moses-like Birth

## The Incarnation of Superman

Superman is sent to earth from the heavens to live as a human man, like Jesus. Jesus is fully man and fully God. Superman is, of course, neither. He is fully Kryptonian, but the Kent family gives him something akin to a human spirit, if not ontologically.

Superman also has close kinship with Earth's yellow sun. It gives Superman his power. Jesus, the Son of God, is frequently associated with the "sun", as well.

# The Miraculous and Pro-Life Birth of Superman

Superman's birth may not have been miraculous, but it was certainly unique. General Zod accused Superman's parents of "heresy" for procreating naturally:

> *General Zod: What have you done?*
>
> *Jor-El: Krypton's first natural birth in centuries. And he will be free, free to forge his own destiny.*
>
> *Zod: Heresy. Destroy it.*

Krypton had instituted selective and eugenic-like breeding policies long ago. These policies sound similar to China's "one child" policy.

All the children on Krypton, except Kal-El, were genetically engineered to a pre-determined purpose and thus artificially created through artificial insemination.

General Zod even uses religious phrasing to condemn the natural birth: heresy. Again, the bad guy is saying the bad things, unlike most movies. Natural birth is truth and orthodoxy, as opposed to the heresy of artificial insemination.

## General Zod as King Herod ... and Pharaoh ... and Satan

Note how General Zod finds new purpose in killing the baby. It is a purpose which will propel him on a journey across the stars. This is much like King Herod who searched for Jesus. Herod slaughtered the innocents of Israel to find and kill the baby king, Jesus.

General Zod is also the Satan figure. Zod is the angel who was cast down or exiled from Heaven (Krypton) for making war in Heaven. St. Michael the Archangel, however, would be the general of heaven's forces, not Lucifer.

## Superman Set Adrift Like Moses

Jesus is, of course, the new Moses. Moses was set adrift in the river by his mother to save him from Pharaoh's order to strangle the babies of the Hebrew slaves, for they had become too numerous. Moses was found and adopted by new parents and raised as their own.

Likewise, Superman is set adrift in the universe to be saved from the destruction of Krypton, as well as the pharaoh-figure, General Zod. Super-baby is also adopted by new parents, the Kents, and raised as their own.

This makes sense since Superman's original creators, Jerry Siegel and Joe Shuster, were Jewish. Here's an article from FoxNews making this exact point:

When Jerry Siegel and Joe Shuster created their iconic comic book hero Superman in 1938, their character wasn't just a representation of "Truth, Justice and the American Way," but for many, a metaphor for Jewish immigrants in 1930s America. Created by two young Jewish men, Superman was an allusion to the Jewish faith and history, from his baby Moses-like origins to his golem-esque invincibility, to his outcast status, and his ultimate struggle to assimilate in a new land.

# Superman is like Moses and Adam: he Skull Codex

This may be the coolest connection between Jesus and Superman in all of *Man of Steel*, *Batman v. Superman*, and *Justice League*.

Jesus wasn't just the New Moses. Jesus was also the New Adam. Adam was the forefather of the entire human race by blood, likewise Jesus, by his blood, redeems the whole human race.

Remember the skull that Jor-El steals from Krypton?

That skull is the Kryptonian citizen registry growth codex (or simply the codex). The skull was the remains of an ancient Kryptonian that contained the potential genetic information of all Kryptonians. The skull bore the genetic blueprint of the entire Kryptonian race.

It was the skull of the Kryptonian Adam! The codex was to be used in conjunction with Kryptonian GENESIS chambers. Yes, Genesis, as in the Book of Adam and Eve.

The Codex held the genetic attributes of all artificially incubated infants before their inception. Jor-El stored all the Codex's information in the body of Kal-El, the last known survivor of Krypton.

... Therefore, Superman was the New Adam of Krypton, just as Jesus is the New Adam of the human race. This is an amazingly deep connection between Superman and Jesus.

One more thing ...

There is also a connection between Jesus and Adam's skull. Where was Jesus crucified? Golgotha, the "place of the skull" in Hebrew. Mt. Calvary, or "skull", in Greek. Whose skull was it?

... It was ADAM's skull!

# Similarities in the Life of Superman and Jesus

## The Age of Superman

What is the age of Superman when he begins his "public ministry"? 33 is the age of Kal-El when he performs his first public miracles. Of course, that's not the age Jesus began his public ministry, but the year of his crucifixion.

Jesus' public ministry likely lasted three years, so 30 would have been the more Jesus-like age, BUT a lot of things happen in Man of Steel. Superman basically begins his public ministry and gives up his life all at 33, so it still works.

## The Hidden Years of Superman and Jesus

Superman, like Jesus, had a Messianic secret. Jesus often implored people to keep his gifts of healing and his Messianic mission a secret. Take the following the Gospel of Mark, chapter 8:

"Who do men say that I am?" And they told him, "John the Baptist; and others say, Eli'jah; and others one of the prophets." And he asked them, "But who do you say that I am?" Peter answered him, "You are the Christ." And he charged them to tell no one about him.

Likewise, Jonathan Kent, played by Kevin Costner below, told young Clark to keep his powers a secret. Jonathan Kent, below, is telling Clark not to save him from the oncoming tornado. Superman's foster father dies to protect Superman's Messianic secret.

Speaking of Jonathan Kent ...

## Superman's St. Joseph: Jonathan Kent, His Adopted Father

Jonathan Kent (Kevin Costner), Clark Kent's adoptive father, is like Jesus' adoptive dad, Saint Joseph. Both foster fathers are tradesmen. Saint Joseph is a carpenter. Jonathan is a farmer and a mechanic, working with his hands (and reminding me of Field of Dreams).

Superman's ship or flying "manger", if you will, is even kept in the Kents' stable.

By the time of Jesus' public ministry, we no longer hear about St. Joseph. As in the case of Jonathan Kent, many Biblical scholars believe that St. Joseph has already died.

## Jesus and Superman are both the Salvation of Mankind

Both of Superman's fathers, Jor-El and Jonathan Kent, talk about Superman's salvific mission and destiny. Here is Jor-El speaking about this in Man of Steel:

Here is another quote from Jor-El on the salvation to be wrought by Superman:

*You will give the people an ideal to strive towards. They will race behind you, they will stumble, they will fall. But in time, they will join you in the sun. In time, you will help them accomplish wonders.*

Jonathan Kent speaks to how Superman will lead humanity

to new heights by his example, as well:

> *You're not just anyone. One day, you're going to
> have to make a choice. You'll have to decide what
> kind of man you want to grow up to be. Whoever
> that man is, good character or bad, he's going to
> change the world.*

## The Justice League and the Apostles of Jesus; Batman as Saint Peter

The Justice League is like Superman's apostles. Superman's powers are extraordinary, even among the Justice League.

Batman, of course, is the one who actually goes around gathering up the other meta-humans, like Wonder Woman, the Flash, and Aquaman. Batman, however, speaks of Superman in Messianic terms.

Superman, was a beacon to the world.

Batman is like St. Peter, gathering the Church together after the death of Jesus (and the death of Superman).

Aquaman is even a "fisherman" of sorts like Saints Peter and Andrew. Of course, he also wields a trident like Poseidon, even made from the "Poseidon metal", as we are told in the Aquaman movie. This makes a connection between Superman and Zeus.

# Similarities in the Deaths and Resurrections of Superman and Jesus [SPOILERS]

## The Sacrifice (Passion) of Superman

Superman is always being called on to sacrifice himself, as Jesus did on the Cross. There are several moments through the Man of Steel, Batman v. Superman, and Justice League when Superman is depicted in a cruciform or cross-like posture:

[SPOILER ALERT] Superman wields a spear against Doomsday. Conversely, a spear is used to pierce the side of Jesus on the Cross.

## Both Jesus and Superman and Resurrected

[SPOILERS] After Superman's death in *Batman v. Superman*, the Justice League resurrects Superman using the "Mother Box" in an amniotic chamber aboard the Kryptonian ship. Jesus is also resurrected, obviously, but by the power of God, not his friends.

Superman does a number on his friends after his "Pet Sematary" Resurrection:

There is a giant burst of energy following Superman's resurrection. This is similar to the giant burst of energy that created the Shroud of Turin when Jesus was resurrected and still laying in the tomb.

# Some Last Notes on the Superman-Jesus Connections:

## Superman and the Bullies

The Gnostic Gospels, written long after the actual Gospel, depict Jesus striking down a bully and then healing him. I believe something like this is also depicted in the Protoevangelium of St. James.

## Superman is Catholic

When things get tough, Clark Kent seeks advice from a priest. Visible in the background is a large painting of Jesus so you can see Supes and Christ side-by-side.

## Jesus and Superman's Doomsday

Jesus' Second Coming will coincide with Armageddon or "Doomsday". Also, one of Superman's chief villains is "Doomsday". This is the Lex Luthor-created "big bad" of *Batman v. Superman*.

## General Zod Admonished Like St. Peter

Jesus admonishes Saint Peter after Peter cuts off the ear of the temple servant Malchus: "Those who live by the sword will die by the sword". Likewise, Jor-El says to General Zod:

> *You've taken up the sword...*
> *...against your own people.*

# About the Author

Scott Smith is a Catholic author, attorney, and theologian. He and his wife Ashton are the parents of four wild-eyed children and live in their hometown of New Roads, Louisiana.

Smith is currently serving as the Chairman of the Men of the Immaculata, the Grand Knight of his local Knights of Columbus council, and a co-host of the Catholic Nerds Podcast. Smith has served as a minister and teacher far and wide: from Angola, Louisiana's maximum security prison, to the slums of Kibera, Kenya.

Smith is the author of the first pro-life horror novel, *The Seventh Word*. His other books include *Pray the Rosary with St. Pope John Paul II, The Catholic ManBook, Everything You Need to Know About Mary But Were Never Taught*, and *Blessed is He Who …* (Biographies of Blesseds).

Scott regularly contributes to his blog, "The Scott Smith Blog" at www.thescottsmithblog.com, WINNER of the 2018-2019 Fisher's Net Award for Best Catholic Blog:

Scott's other books can be found at his publisher's, Holy Water Books, website, holywaterbooks.com, as well as on Amazon.

His other books on theology and the Catholic faith include *The Catholic ManBook, Everything You Need to Know About Mary But Were Never Taught*, and *Blessed is He Who …* (Biographies of Blesseds). More on these below …

His fiction includes *The Seventh Word*, a pro-life horror novel, and the *Cajun Zombie Chronicles*, the Catholic version of the zombie apocalypse.

# Pray, Hope, & Don't Worry:
# Catholic Prayer Journal for Women

Scott also recently authored a series of prayer journals with his wife. *The Pray, Hope, & Don't Worry* Prayer Journal to Overcome Stress and Anxiety:

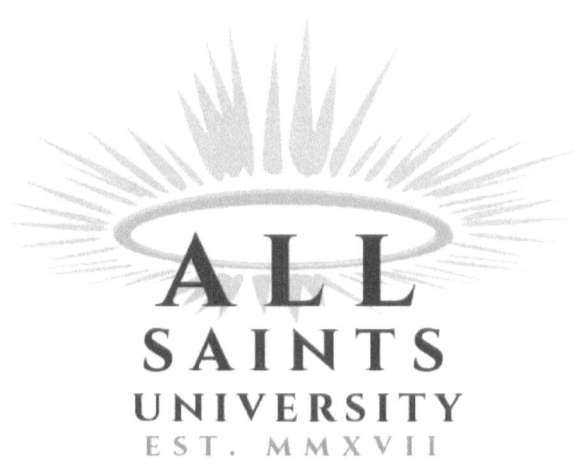

**ALL**
**SAINTS**
**UNIVERSITY**
EST. MMXVII

Scott has also produced courses on the Blessed Mother and Scripture for All Saints University.

Learn about the Blessed Mary from anywhere and learn to defend your mother! It includes over six hours of video plus a free copy of the next book ... Enroll Now!

What You *Need* to Know About Mary
But Were Never Taught

# Pray the Rosary
# with St. John Paul II

St. John Paul II said "the Rosary is my favorite prayer." So what could possibly make praying the Rosary even better? Praying the Rosary with St. John Paul II!

This book includes a reflection from John Paul II for every mystery of the Rosary. You will find John Paul II's biblical

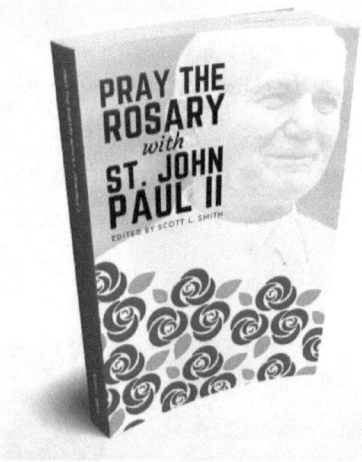

reflections on the twenty mysteries of the Rosary that provide practical insights to help you not only understand the twenty mysteries but also live them.

St. John Paul II said "The Rosary is my favorite prayer. A marvelous prayer! Marvelous in its simplicity and its depth. In the prayer we repeat many times the words that the Virgin Mary heard from the Archangel, and from her kinswoman Elizabeth."

St. John Paul II said "the Rosary is the storehouse of countless blessings." In this new book, he will help you dig even deeper into the treasures contained within the Rosary.

You will also learn St. John Paul II's spirituality of the Rosary: "To pray the Rosary is to hand over our burdens to the merciful hearts of Christ and His mother."

"The Rosary, though clearly Marian in character, is at heart a Christ-centered prayer. It has all the depth of the gospel message in its entirety. It is an echo of the prayer of Mary, her perennial Magnificat for the work of the redemptive Incarnation which began in her virginal womb."

Take the Rosary to a whole new level with St. John Paul the Great! St. John Paul II, *pray for us!*

# Prayer Like a Warrior: Spiritual Combat & War Room Prayer Guide

***Don't get caught unarmed!*** Develop your Prayer Room Strategy and Battle Plan.

An invisible war rages around you. Something or someone is attacking you, unseen, unheard, yet felt throughout every aspect of your life. An army of demons under the banner of Satan has a singular focus: your destruction and that of everyone you know and love.

You need to protect your soul, your heart, your mind, your marriage, your children, your relationships, your resolve, your dreams, and your destiny.

Do you want to be a Prayer Warrior, but don't know where to start? The Devil's battle plan depends on catching you unarmed and unaware. If you're tired of being pushed around and wrecked by sin and distraction, this book is for you.

Do you feel uncomfortable speaking to God? Do you struggle with distractions in the presence of Almighty God? Praying to God may feel foreign, tedious, or like a ritual, and is He really listening? What if He never hears, never responds? This book will show you that God always listens and always answers.

In this book, you will learn how to prayer effectively no matter where you are mentally, what your needs are, or how you are feeling:

- Prayers when angry or your heart is troubled
- Prayers for fear, stress, and hopelessness
- Prayers to overcome pride, unforgiveness, and bitterness
- Prayers for rescue and shelter

Or are you looking to upgrade your prayer life? This book is for you, too. You already know that a prayer war room is a powerful weapon in spiritual warfare. Prepare for God to pour out blessings on your life.

Author, theologian, and attorney Scott L. Smith, Jr. has tested the prayers and wisdom of this book as a missionary in Africa, a minister in maximum security prisons, in the courtroom, and, most challenging of all, as a husband and father of four.

Our broken world and broken souls need the prayers and direction found in this book. Don't waste time fumbling through your prayer life. Pray more strategically when you have a War Room Battle Plan. Jesus showed His disciples how to pray and He wants to show you how to pray, too.

# Catholic Nerds Podcast

As you might have noticed, Scott is obviously well-credentialed as a nerd. Check out Scott's podcast: the Catholic Nerds Podcast on iTunes, Podbean, Google Play, and wherever good podcasts are found!

# What You Need to Know About Mary But Were Never Taught

Give a robust defense of the Blessed Mother using Scripture. Now, more than ever, every Catholic needs to learn how to defend their mother, the Blessed Mother. Because now, more than ever, the family is under attack and needs its Mother.

Discover the love story, hidden within the whole of Scripture, of the Father for his daughter, the Holy Spirit for his spouse, and the Son for his MOTHER.

This collection of essays and the All Saints University course made to accompany it will demonstrate through Scripture how the Immaculate Conception of Mary was prophesied in Genesis.

It will also show how the Virgin Mary is the New Eve, the New Ark, and the New Queen of Israel.

# The Catholic ManBook

Do you want to reach Catholic Man LEVEL: EXPERT? *The Catholic ManBook* is your handbook to achieving Sainthood, manly Sainthood. Find the following resources inside, plus many others:

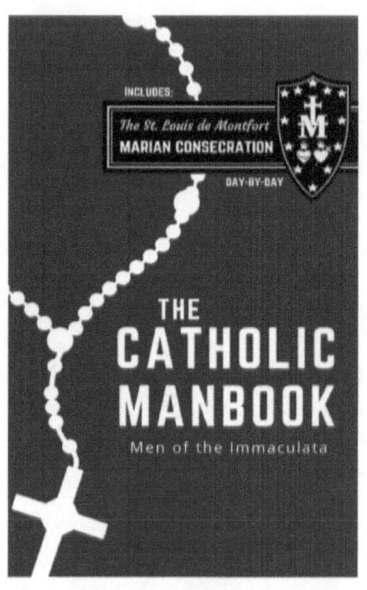

- Top Catholic Apps, Websites, and Blogs
- Everything you need to pray the Rosary
- The Most Effective Daily Prayers & Novenas, including the Emergency Novena
- Going to Confession and Eucharistic Adoration like a boss!
- Mastering the Catholic Liturgical Calendar

*The Catholic ManBook* contains the collective wisdom of The Men of the Immaculata, of saints, priests and laymen, fathers and sons, single and married. Holiness is at your fingertips. Get your copy today.

This edition also includes a revised and updated St. Louis de Montfort Marian consecration. Follow the prayers in a day-by-day format.

# The Seventh Word
### *The FIRST Pro-Life Horror Novel!*

Pro-Life hero, Abby Johnson, called it "legit scary ... I don't like reading this as night! ... It was good, it was so good ... it was terrifying, but good."

The First Word came with Cain, who killed the first child of man. The Third Word was Pharaoh's instruction to the midwives. The Fifth Word was carried from Herod to Bethlehem. One of the Lost Words dwelt among the Aztecs and hungered after their children.

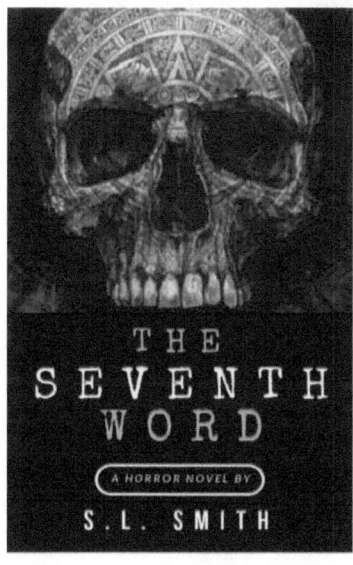

Evil hides behind starched white masks. The ancient Aztec demon now conducts his affairs in the sterile environment of corporate medical facilities. An insatiable hunger draws the demon to a sleepy Louisiana hamlet.

There, it contracts the services of a young attorney, Jim David, whose unborn child is the ultimate object of the demon's designs. Monsignor, a mysterious priest of unknown age and origin, labors unseen to save the soul of a small town hidden deep within Louisiana's plantation country, nearly forgotten in a bend of the Mississippi River.

You'll be gripped from start to heart-stopping finish in this page-turning thriller.

With roots in Bram Stoker's Dracula, this horror novel reads like Stephen King's classic stories of towns being slowly devoured by an unseen evil and the people who unite against it.

The book is set in southern Louisiana, an area the author brings to life with compelling detail based on his local knowledge.

# Blessed is He Who ...
# Models of Catholic Manhood

You are the average of the five people you spend the most time with, so spend more time with the Saints! Here are several men that you need to get to know whatever your age or station in life. These short biographies will give you an insight into how to live better, however you're living.

**From Kings to computer nerds**, old married couples to single teenagers, these men gave us extraordinary examples of holiness:

- Pier Giorgio Frassati & Carlo Acutis – Here are two extraordinary **young men**, an athlete and a computer nerd, living on either side of the 20th Century
- Two men of royal stock, Francesco II and Archduke Eugen, lived lives of holiness despite all the world conspiring against them.
- There's also the **simple husband and father**, Blessed Luigi. Though he wasn't a king, he can help all of us treat the women in our lives as queens.

*Blessed Is He Who ... Models of Catholic Manhood* explores the lives of six men who found their greatness in Christ and His Bride, the Church. In six succinct chapters, the authors, noted historian Brian J. Costello and theologian and attorney Scott L. Smith, share with you the uncommon lives of exceptional men who will one day be numbered among the Saints of Heaven, men who can bring all of us closer to sainthood.

# THANKS FOR READING!
## *TOTUS TUUS*

www.ingramcontent.com/pod-product-compliance
Lightning Source LLC
Chambersburg PA
CBHW030542130626
46552CB00006B/2373